BUBBE & GRAM

My Two Grandmothers

Written by Joan C. Hawxhurst
Illustrated by Jane K. Bynum

Dovetail Publishing, Inc.
P.O. Box 19945
Kalamazoo, MI 49019
(616) 342-2900
dovetail@mich.com

Book design by Grafika Design, Oak Park, IL.
Published by Dovetail Publishing, Kalamazoo, MI.
Printed in the U.S.A.

Library of Congress Cataloging-in-Publication Data
Hawxhurst, Joan Clair
Bubbe and Gram: My Two Grandmothers / written by
Joan C. Hawxhurst, illustrated by Jane K. Bynum.
— first edition.
p. cm.
Summary: A young child learns about Christianity and Judaism from her two very different grandmothers.
ISBN 0-9651284-2-3
1. Grandparents—Juvenile literature.
2. Children and religion—mixed heritages—Juvenile literature.
3. Judaism—customs and practices—Juvenile literature.
4. Christianity—customs and practices—Juvenile literature.
I. Bynum, Jane K., ill.
II. Title

In my family, I have two grandmothers. They each have a different religion.

My dad's mother is Jewish.
I call her Bubbe.

My mom's mother is Christian.
I call her Gram.

At Bubbe's house, there's a special prayer-holder on her door. It's called a mezuzah, and inside is a special Jewish prayer called the Shema. Sometimes Bubbe says the Shema out loud to me.

Hear, O Israel: the Lord our God, the Lord is one!

At Gram's house, there is a special picture on her wall. It's a picture of a man called Jesus, and it has words written underneath. Sometimes Gram says the Lord's Prayer out loud to me. *Our Father who art in Heaven, hallowed be thy name.*

Sometimes I go to Bubbe's house for Friday night dinner, after we go to temple together. It's a special time called Shabbat. We light candles, say blessings, and eat braided challah bread.

Sometimes I go to Gram's house for Sunday dinner, after we go to church together. It's a special time when we have a big meal in the middle of the day. We put out the fancy dishes and say grace before we eat.

I like it when Bubbe tells me stories. She tells me about baby Moses floating down the Nile in a basket, and about grown-up Moses receiving commandments from God. She tells me about the Maccabees fighting for their temple. She tells me how Moses and the Maccabees saw miracles happen.

I like it when Gram tells me stories. She tells me about baby Jesus being born in a stable. She tells me about grown-up Jesus helping people who were lonely or sick and teaching people to love each other. She tells me how Jesus saw miracles happen.

When I visit Bubbe at Passover, we have a special dinner called a seder. Bubbe says that at Passover we are celebrating freedom. We dip eggs in salt water. We eat flat bread called matzah. After we eat, I get to search for the hidden afikomen.

When I visit Gram on Easter Sunday, we have a special dinner there, too. Gram says that at Easter we are celebrating springtime and Jesus coming back to be with us in the world. We dip eggs in colored dyes. We wear our fancy Easter clothes. After we eat, I get to hunt for Easter eggs.

At Chanukah time, Bubbe helps me light the candles on the menorah—one more each night for eight nights. We make potato latkes, sing songs, and play dreidel with chocolate money called gelt.

At Christmas time, Gram helps me turn on the colored lights on her tree. We decorate cookies and sing Christmas carols, and Gram lets me play with the little stable with baby Jesus inside.

There are lots of things that are different about Bubbe and Gram. Sometimes Bubbe doesn't understand the things I tell her about Gram's house. She says that's because she grew up practicing a different religion. But she always tells me that it's good to learn about being Christian.

Sometimes Gram doesn't understand the things I tell her about Bubbe's house. She says that's because she grew up practicing a different religion. But she always tells me that it's good to learn about being Jewish.

I love Bubbe, and she loves me. It's fun to learn from her about being Jewish.

I love Gram, and she loves me. It's fun to learn from her about being Christian.

I am really lucky to have my Bubbe and Gram.